To:

From:

On my journey to see,
who exactly I'll be.
Oh, the friends I will help.
and the places I'll see.

Step by step.
Hop by hop.
Helping when I can,
until I reach the top!

Hopping through the forest,
I heard a big yell.
"Help!" Lizzie hollered.
"I have lost my tail!"

With a wave of my wand,
and a wiggle of my ear,
Lizzie felt a tingle,
and her tail reappeared!

Step by step.
Hop by hop.
Helping when I can,
until I reach the top!

Floating in the pond,
I heard a loud shout.
"Help!" cried Scottie.
"I'm stuck and can't get out!"

With a wave of my wand,
and a tap of my knee,
Scottie felt a tingle,
and he sprang out free!

Step by step.
Hop by hop.
Helping when I can,
until I reach the top!

Basking in the sunlight,
I heard a sad plea.
"Help!" called Susie.
"My nest fell from the tree!"

With a wave of my wand,
and a tip of my hat,
next came a poof!
Susie had her nest back!

Step by step.
Hop by hop.
Helping when I can,
until I reach the top!

Oh, the places I've been,
helping all of my friends,
They've got troubles at the start,
but I'll solve them in the end!

Step by step.

Hop by hop.

To be continued...

First edition July 2020

ISBN 978-1-7351705-5-8 (hardback)
ISBN 978-1-7351705-4-1 (paperback)
ISBN 978-1-7351705-3-4 (ebook)

www.linusthewizard.com